SCELIDOSAURUS
(ske-LI-doh-SAW-rus)

TYRANNOSAURUS
(tie-RAN-oh-SAW-rus)

TRICERATOPS
(try-SER-a-tops)

STEGOSAURUS
(STEG-oh-SAW-rus)

PTERODACTYL
(TER-oh-DAC-til)

APATOSAURUS
(a-PAT-oh-SAW-rus)

ANCHISAURUS
(AN-ki-SAW-rus)

In memory of Mason Jones and for all of his friends
at Deri Primary School, Bargoed, who miss him very much—I.W.

For Calum—A.R.

Text copyright © 2006 by Ian Whybrow
Illustrations copyright © 2006 by Adrian Reynolds
All rights reserved. Published in the United States by Random House Children's Books, a division of Random House, Inc., New York.
First published in 2006 by Puffin Books, a division of the Penguin Group, 80 Strand, London, WC2R 0RL, England.
RANDOM HOUSE and colophon are registered trademarks of Random House, Inc.
www.randomhouse.com/kids
Library of Congress Cataloging-in-Publication Data
Whybrow, Ian. Harry and the dinosaurs go to school /
Ian Whybrow ; illustrated by Adrian Reynolds. — 1st American ed.
p. cm.
SUMMARY: On Harry's first day at his new school he is not sure whether or not to bring his bucket of dinosaurs,
but in the end the dinosaurs help him make a friend.
ISBN: 978-0-375-84180-4 (trade)
[1. First day of school—Fiction. 2. Schools—Fiction. 3. Dinosaurs—Fiction. 4. Toys—Fiction.]
I. Reynolds, Adrian, ill. II. Title.
PZ7.W6225Hans 2007 [E]—dc22
2006025438
MANUFACTURED IN CHINA
10 9 8 7 6 5 4 3 2 1   First American Edition

Harry and the Dinosaurs Go to School

Ian Whybrow and Adrian Reynolds

Random House   New York

It was a big day for Harry. He was starting at his new school.
He was very excited because one of his friends, Charlie, was
starting that day, too.

Stegosaurus said he didn't want to go. Not after Triceratops
told him that there were no "Raahhs" allowed in class.
Mom said not to worry—school would be fine.

Harry blew his whistle. Then, just like a teacher, he said, "In twos, holding hands, my dinosaurs. No talking and jump in the bucket."

All the dinosaurs did what Harry said. All except Stegosaurus. He was so nervous, all his plates were rattling. Harry had to give him a special hug.

Sam said, "You can't take dinosaurs to school, silly!"
That's why her toast fell on the floor.

Mom took Harry to school.

Mrs. Rance was waiting at the classroom door when Harry and Mom got there.

"Hello, Harry," she said. "Welcome to your new school."

Harry said goodbye to Mom, and Mrs. Rance showed
Harry the coat pegs.

"You can leave your lunchbox here, too," she said.

Harry was too shy to ask if he could bring his bucket,
and that's why his dinosaurs got left outside the classroom.

Harry missed his dinosaurs, so he didn't like the classroom, or the art corner, or his special work tray.

And he felt sorry for another new boy with a digger who cried when his mom went home. The boy wouldn't say one single word. Not even his name.

Harry sort of liked the playground at playtime.
But even the monkey bars were not much fun
without his dinosaurs.

Back in class, the digger boy still wouldn't speak.
"Maybe he wants to go to the bathroom," Harry
suggested. "Can I show him where it is?"

Mrs. Rance said, "Good idea. That's very nice of
you, Harry."

All the way to the bathroom, the boy kept quiet.
It was the same on the way back, till they got to the
coats. Then they heard a voice, very sad and very soft.
"Raaaaaaaaaaaaaahh!" it said.

"That's my dinosaurs," said Harry. "They miss me.
Would you like to meet them?"
The boy nodded.
So Harry said, "This is my Apatosaurus and my
Anchisaurus and my Scelidosaurus."

"This is Triceratops and Tyrannosaurus. Pterodactyl is the baby. Wait! Where's Stegosaurus?"

"Jump out, Stegosaurus," called Harry. "Don't be shy!"

But Stegosaurus wanted to whisper something in Harry's ear.

"Ah," said Harry. "Stegosaurus says he will only come out if he can have a ride on your digger."

And do you know what? The boy nodded and passed it over.

When Harry and the boy got back, Mrs. Rance said,
"Oh, good! Dinosaurs! I love dinosaurs. Do they 'Raaahh'?"

"RAAAAAAAAAAAAHH!" said the dinosaurs, and blew all the windows open.

"My goodness!" said Mrs. Rance. "That *was* a 'Raaahh'!"

They all sat down in the classroom.
"Now we are going to make new labels for our coat pegs," said Mrs. Rance. "Who knows how to write their name? Hands up."

The boy with the digger put up his hand.

"And what are you going to write?" said Mrs. Rance with a smile.

"Jackosaurus!" said the boy.

It was the very first word he had spoken all day. And what a good joke, too!

All the other children laughed and laughed.

Harry felt very happy.
He and his new friend sat down together at a
table with the dinosaurs and Charlie.

They laughed and they "Raaahhed" and they
made beautiful labels to show where they belonged.

ENDOSAURUS

SCELIDOSAURUS
(ske-LI-doh-SAW-rus)

TYRANNOSAURUS
(tie-RAN-oh-SAW-rus)

TRICERATOPS
(try-SER-a-tops)

STEGOSAURUS
(STEG-oh-SAW-rus)

PTERODACTYL
(TER-oh-DAC-til)

APATOSAURUS
(a-PAT-oh-SAW-rus)

ANCHISAURUS
(AN-ki-SAW-rus)